001

TW ENTY

MINI

02029

DEMCO

TWENTY

 MINI

MYSTERIES

You Can Solve

Dina Anastasio

**Illustrated by
Kevin Faeber**

Hippo

Scholastic Children's Books,
Scholastic Ltd,
Commonwealth House, 1-19 New Oxford Street,
London WC1A 1NU, UK

Published in the UK by Scholastic Ltd, 1996

Text copyright © Dina Anastasio, 1996

Illustrations © Kevin Faeber, 1996

ISBN 0 590 13389 6

Printed and bound in Great Britain
by Cox & Wyman Ltd, Reading, Berkshire

10 9 8 7 6 5 4 3 2 1

CONTENTS

1. SURPRISE!

I'll start at the beginning. The next day was my birthday. I was going to be ten years old. After I was ten, I would be able to stay up later. If I was lucky, I would be riding a bigger bike. I would be able to play soccer with the bigger kids. I couldn't wait.

I couldn't sleep at all that night. I just lay there in my bed and stared at the moon. It was full and bright, and it was shining right into my eyes. But that wasn't what was keeping me awake. Tomorrow I would be ten years old. *That* was why I couldn't sleep.

I tossed and turned for a few hours, and then I got up. I turned on the light. I tried to read a book, but the words didn't mean anything at all. All I could think about was the racing bike that I might get for my birthday. I wondered if they had bought a red one. I had forgotten to ask for a red one. But that is what I wanted.

I wondered if they had bought me a bike at all. Maybe they didn't have enough money. Maybe they didn't want me to have a fast bike.

I turned off the light and tried to go to sleep again. But it was no use. Important thoughts kept zipping in and out of the corners of my brain. Would I get the bike? Would they have a party for me? Who would come? What would they bring me? Would I have a cake? Would it be chocolate?

At midnight I gave up and got out of bed. In a few hours everybody would be up and I could have breakfast. Would they give me the bike at breakfast, or would I have to wait until after school? Maybe I'd have to wait until supper. By supper I would be too tired to ride it.

I went down to the kitchen and poured myself a glass of milk. Then I found a packet of biscuits and carried everything into the sitting room. I turned on the telly and flicked the channels, but there was nothing on. Just boring old chat shows. So I ate the biscuits and drank the milk and turned the telly off.

I still wasn't tired, but I couldn't think of anything to do. I had never been up so late before. Everybody was asleep, so there was no one to talk to. I couldn't go outside and play with my friends.

I was bored. I was very, very bored.

And then I had an idea. I would search the house. I would pretend that I was a policewoman looking for a bank robber. I would pretend that the robber was

hiding somewhere in my house.

I started in the attic. I had to tiptoe so as not to wake anybody up, but that was easy for me. I'm little for my age, so I don't make much noise. I pulled the light string in the attic and looked around. Maybe the robber was hiding in that big trunk in the corner. Or maybe the robber was hiding behind the boxes of old baby clothes.

I searched everywhere, but the robber wasn't in there. I was feeling pretty brave, until I remembered that there wasn't really a robber at all. So I turned off the light and went downstairs. I searched the bathroom, but I didn't go into my parents' room because I didn't want to wake them up. And I didn't go into my brother's room either, because I knew he'd be mad if I did.

After I'd searched the kitchen, I went down into the basement. It was scary going down the stairs; dark and shadowy and strange. But I was a brave policewoman and I carried on.

I felt a spider's web brush my face as I made my way down the steps. But that didn't stop me. The robber was waiting down there somewhere, and I was going to find him.

It was even darker at the bottom of the steps. I knew there was a lamp on the other side of the basement, so I made my way over there. I couldn't see a thing. It was creepy and very scary. But I made it.

And then it happened! Just as I reached for the lamp and flicked it on, I knocked something over. The *something* was in my way. It was big, and it made a very loud noise when it crashed to the floor.

The room was bright with light now, and I could see the thing that I had knocked over.

The thing was a shiny red racing bike!

I swung around and gasped. There were *Happy Birthday* signs hanging everywhere. Balloons floated from the ceiling. Forks and knives and party decorations covered the table.

But the most interesting thing of all was the sign that stretched from one side of the room to the other.

The sign said *SURPRISE!*

I knew I shouldn't be down there, so I turned off the lamp quickly. I raced to the steps and bounded up them two at a time. But I wasn't fast enough. Suddenly, the basement door opened and my father's voice said, "Who's there?"

"It's just me. I couldn't sleep."

"You've seen your surprise," he said sadly.

"What surprise?" I asked quickly. I didn't want to spoil his fun.

"You mean you haven't seen it?"

"No, no," I assured him. "I was just on my way down when I heard a crash. I didn't even get a chance to turn on the lamp."

"Well, go into the kitchen while I see what the crash was," he said.

I pretended to go back into the kitchen, but I didn't really. I just stomped a few times and stayed at the top of the steps. He couldn't see me, because the lamp was around the corner. But I could see the room from where I was.

I heard him walk across the room. I heard him trip over the bike. Then I heard him touch the lamp.

He touched it and said, "Ow! I've burned my hand!" And then he flicked it on.

When the room was light, he picked up the bike and leant it against the wall. Then he looked around for a minute and turned the lamp off again. I raced into the kitchen and waited for him there.

"Well," he said, when he came in. "You've seen your surprise."

I didn't know what to say, so I didn't say anything for a while. Finally I said, "It's my birthday right now, so I guess it's all right. But how did you know I'd seen it?"

"Oh, something shed a little light on it," he laughed.

How did he know that I'd seen my surprise party?

2. REMOTE CONTROL

It all began when I was messing around with the old remote control. I picked it up by mistake and pointed it at the telly. I pushed the *ON* button, but nothing happened. I pushed the button again, but still nothing happened. That was when I realized it was the wrong remote. That remote had been broken for months.

I turned on the telly with the good remote and sat back. It was a boring show, so I started fiddling with the broken remote for something to do. First I broke open the case. Then I looked at the inside for a long time. I'm ten years old and I know a lot about how things work, but I had never seen wires like these. After a while, I started playing with the wires. I hooked a red wire to a green wire, and then I tied two white wires together.

When I was finished, I put the case back on and pointed the remote at the telly. I pushed the OFF button, but nothing happened. But when I pushed the button marked 1, the whole picture changed. Suddenly, the show that I had been watching turned black and white. All the colours disappeared.

It was the strangest thing. One minute there was colour, and the next minute it was gone. I tried the 1 button again, and the colour returned.

So, I thought. The button marked 1 controls the colour.

My dog, Lady, watched me as I played with the 1 button. I guess she didn't like all that flickering, because she started to bark. She barked really loud, so I turned around and told her to stop. But she just barked louder. And then something really strange happened. Lady's mouth was open, as if she was barking, but no sound was coming out.

I looked down at the remote. I had been pointing it at Lady and pushing buttons. But which one had I pushed?

Somehow I had muted her! Somehow I had made her silent! But how?

My mother came in and looked down at Lady. "What's the matter with the dog?" she asked.

I hid the remote behind my back. "I don't know," I lied.

She flicked off the telly and told me to do my homework. I didn't feel like doing my homework. Maybe the remote could do it for me. Maybe if I pushed the numbers

385 or 223, all my homework would be done.

I tried it, but it didn't work. When I pushed those buttons, nothing happened.

I sat in the sitting room and did my homework. My older brother Liam was sitting in a chair by the window, facing my mother. My little brother Stan was on the floor in the corner. I was lying on the sofa. We were all doing our homework, except for my mother, of course.

I must have been playing with the remote while I was working, because suddenly my mother said, "Put that away, Jimmy."

I was watching an ant, so I didn't really hear her the first time she said it. The ant was crawling around on the other side of the room. I pointed the remote at it and pushed *12*. Suddenly, the strangest thing of all happened. The ant started to fly.

"Put that away!" my mother said again. I could tell that she hadn't seen the ant. She just wanted me to do my homework.

I dropped the remote onto the floor and went into the kitchen. One of my brothers was right behind me. He had seen the ant fly.

"How did you *do* that?" he cried.

"How old are you?" I mumbled, as I stuffed some cake into my mouth.

He looked at me as if I was crazy. But then he under-

stood and left the kitchen.

When I came back into the sitting room, the remote was gone. My brothers were sitting where they had been before. And believe it or not, my mother was flying above her chair.

"Put me down!" she shouted. "Get me down from here!"

I searched for the remote, but I couldn't find it. One of my brothers must have had it. But which one?

I had to hurry. What if he pointed the remote at me? What if he pushed 12 and I started to fly? That might be fun, but I wanted to know what number to push to *stop* flying first. What if he pushed a different number? What if he pushed 543 or 897 and I turned into a toad? What if he changed me into a sink or a cuckoo clock? What if I started oinking or mooing?

I had to get that remote back! I had to get it back now!

I studied my brothers. They were both doing their homework. But I knew one of them had the remote, somewhere. I watched them carefully. And then I remembered.

Suddenly, I lunged! I threw myself at my brother and found the remote next to him.

I pointed it at my mother and pushed 12 again. But nothing happened. I tried some other numbers, but still nothing happened. And then I had a brilliant idea.

I pushed *21!*

It worked. My mother floated down and landed in her chair. She stared at me and growled softly, like a cheetah whose cubs are in danger.

She bared her teeth and threw herself at me. Had I turned her into a wild animal? I dropped the remote and covered my face. I waited. In a second she would tear me apart. But nothing happened.

I opened my eyes and peeked at her. She was standing in the middle of the room with the remote in her hand. She looked at it and growled again. Then she dropped it and raised her foot. Without a word, she stamped on it, hard! Then she picked it up and ripped out every single wire.

Suddenly, Lady began to bark. She barked and barked and barked.

My mother must have stamped on the right button.

"That's that then," my mother announced when she was finished. She was back to her old self. She hadn't been a wild animal at all. She had just been angry.

"I didn't do it, Mom!" I said. "I didn't make you fly!"

"I know," she told me. "But I do know who did."

Which brother pushed the buttons
that made their mother fly?

3. ONE SMALL DIFFERENCE

"**Y**ou mean we can do *anything*?" my twin sister, Helen cried. "Anything at *all*? ".

My mother nodded and said, "Yes dear. It's your room and you can do anything you want with it."

When she was gone, Helen started to dance around. I guess she was happy. Helen and I are exactly alike. We look alike. We act alike. We dress alike. And we sound alike. It's great, because no one can ever tell us apart. There is only one thing that is different about us, but I'm not going to tell you what that is.

Not yet.

"What'll we do, Ellen?" Helen asked me.

I had a lot of ideas, but they weren't very good. She had a lot of ideas, but they weren't very good either. But we agreed on one thing. We weren't going to paint the walls grey.

It had been raining for weeks. Every day it rained and rained. The sky was grey. The world was grey.

We needed something to brighten up our lives.

"I know," Helen said. "Why don't we paint a big yellow sun on the ceiling? At least we can pretend the sun is shining."

"That's a wonderful idea!" I agreed. "I'll get the ladder!"

"We should have two ladders," Helen said.

But we didn't have two ladders. We only had one, so that would have to do.

I went down to the basement and brought the ladder upstairs. We set it up in the middle of the room. Then we rode our bikes down to the hardware shop and bought some yellow paint.

I climbed up the ladder first and stood on the top. Helen stood right behind me. It was very hard to paint that way, but we did it. Soon, we almost had a sun.

But then Helen made a mistake. She reached way over and the ladder shook. It tilted. It swayed.

And then it fell.

We landed on top of each other and screamed. We must have screamed very loudly, because our mother came running.

She's nice, so she didn't yell at us. She didn't say, "What were you both doing on that ladder?" or, "Are you two crazy?" She just drove us to the hospital and didn't say a word.

The doctor saw us together. First he looked Helen over. Then he looked me over.

"Well, you've done it again," he said at last.

"What?" we asked together.

"You've both done exactly the same thing. You've both broken an arm. You'll still look alike."

The doctor put a cast on my right arm. Then he put a cast on Helen's right arm.

Everybody laughed when we came out. I guess we looked pretty silly. We were dressed the same. We had the same haircuts. We walked the same. And now we both had casts on our right arms.

When we got home, Mum said, "Please be careful.

And whatever you do, only one person on the ladder at a time."

Well, that was silly. Only one of us would have a reason for going up the ladder. Me!

My sister Helen lay down on her bed and stared up at the ceiling. Outside, the sky was grey. Rain was falling, again. But inside, the sun was almost shining.

"We have to finish it," Helen muttered.

"*We* can't," I said. "But *I* can."

I climbed up the ladder and went to work. In a little while the sun was finished.

It rained the next day, and the day after that, and the day after that. But it didn't matter to us, because the sun was right there – above our heads.

How were Ellen and Helen different?

4. THE GHOST

"This place is *haunted*!" Jamie Peters cried. "I heard him. I mean, I heard *it*. I mean, I heard the ghost! I heard him rattling around all night long! And George heard it, too. Didn't you hear him barking?"

Mrs Peters glanced across the room. Their dog, George, was stretched out on the couch, snoring peacefully. "He looks all right now," she said. "He must have been afraid of the wind, dear. There was a terrible storm in the middle of the night. The windows were rattling like crazy. Didn't you hear it?"

"All I heard was the ghost!" Jamie shouted. "I hate this house!"

George opened one lazy eye. Then he stretched and jumped off the couch. He strolled across the room and disappeared through the flap in the kitchen door.

Jamie and his mother were letting a house by the sea for two weeks. The first week was fine. But then the rattling began. Night after night, the windows shook

24

and the floors creaked.

"It isn't a ghost," his mother said. "That storm has been brewing all week. It was just the wind, dear. Look, the sun is out. Let's finish cleaning the house. Then we'll go down to the sea and build the biggest sand-castle in the whole world."

Jamie nodded and went to work. He dried the dishes, and picked up his toys. Then he swept all the floors very carefully.

"We'll need bowls," his mother said when they were finished. "Bowls of all sizes. Big ones and little ones. This sand castle is going to be wonderful!"

George collected all the bowls he could find. As he was about to leave the house, he noticed George's big bowl on the floor. It was perfect. He picked it up and followed his mother to the door.

"What about the ghost?" Jamie asked.

"What about it?"

"Well, what if he's in there?"

"There is no ghost, Jamie!" Mrs Peters insisted in an annoyed tone.

"Well, maybe we should lock the doors anyway. If he's gone out for a walk, we don't want him to come back in."

Mrs Peters sighed and locked the doors.

By noon, Jamie's sand-castle was huge. Towers rose

from it. Moats snaked around it. Water flowed through it.

While Jamie and his mother were swimming, George came and splashed in the tiny lake that Jamie had dug beside the castle. He sniffed at a twig that Jamie had placed in a tower. He dug a hole on the other side of the moat. Then he strolled happily away.

At two, Jamie and his mother returned to the house. Mrs Peters unlocked the door and went into the bedroom to change her clothes. Jamie carried the bowls into the kitchen and dropped them into the sink. Then he turned and glanced down at the floor.

"*MUM!*" he shouted.

"What's the matter, Jamie?" his mother called.

"It's the *ghost*! The ghost has been here again!"

Mrs Peters came into the kitchen and leant against the wall. "That is ridiculous!" she sighed. "There is no such thing as a ghost, Jamie!"

Jamie pointed towards the middle of the kitchen floor. A round pile of wet sand was resting there. It looked exactly like an upside-down bowl.

"You locked the doors, right?" Jamie said.

"Yes. I locked the doors."

"And the windows were closed because of the storm, right?"

Mrs Peters nodded.

"Then no one could have got in here, right?"

Mrs Peters nodded again.

"Except a ghost!" Jamie said. "I told you there was a

ghost! This floor was clean before we went out. I swept it. And now there's a bowl of sand on it. It had to be a *ghost*! It had to be! It had to be!"

Mrs Peters stared at the sand and frowned. She thought about the locked doors. She thought about the closed windows. She thought about the bowls that Jamie had brought to the beach. She thought for a long time. And then she knew.

"It wasn't a ghost, Jamie," she said. "It was something, or should I say *someone* else."

*Do you know how the bowl of sand could
have got into the kitchen?*

5. THE GOLDFISH

"**D**IANA!"

I opened my eyes and looked at the clock. It was only seven in the morning. Too early. Why was she waking me up so early on a Saturday?

"*DIANA!*" my mother called again. "Come down here!"

I slid out of bed and ran downstairs.

"What happened to the goldfish bowl, Diana?" she asked when I came into the kitchen.

I looked down at the floor and sighed. The goldfish bowl was splattered all over the floor. There must have been a hundred pieces of glass.

I shrugged and glanced up at my mother. I could see that she was angry. "Mum," I said. "I don't know what happened to it."

But she didn't believe me. I could tell by the scowl on her face.

"I told you not to touch that fish, Diana," she said. "I

29

was going to give it to your grandmother for her birthday tomorrow. She's lonely. I thought a fish might keep her company."

"Maybe the cat knocked it over," I suggested.

"And where's the fish?" my mother said, not listening.

I was going to tell her that maybe the cat ate it. But I couldn't say that. I knew where the goldfish was, but I couldn't tell her that either. If I told her where the fish was, then she would know that I broke the bowl. I was going to hide the goldfish until the next day. And then I was going to buy a new bowl.

Suddenly I had an idea. I'd make it into a game, and then maybe she wouldn't be so angry.

"All right," I said. "I admit it. I broke the bowl and I know where the goldfish is. Try and guess where it is. I'll give you three guesses."

"I don't *want* three guesses," my mother said. "I just want the goldfish."

"Here's a clue, Mum. The goldfish is hiding in something wet."

"Well, I should hope so," she sighed. "Or it would be dead."

"Come on then," I said. "You've got three guesses."

I could see that Mum was starting to enjoy this. She was thinking.

"Well, all right. Is it in the sink?"

"No, Mum. It's not in the sink."

"Is it in another bowl?" she asked.

"No," I told her.

"Then it must be in the bath."

She was right. I had left the fish in the bathtub overnight, but I didn't want to tell her yet. I wanted to play the game some more. Maybe I'd give her three more guesses.

"It's not in the bath," I lied.

She was starting to get angry again. "This is silly," she said. "We're going down to the shop right now to buy a new bowl for grandma. We'll find the fish later. Now go and get dressed."

"But the shop isn't open yet," I reminded her.

"Then we'll go out for breakfast first."

I went upstairs to get dressed. While I was dressing, I began to feel guilty about lying to her. I should have told her that the fish was in the bath. I decided to move it before we left.

I sneaked downstairs and got a glass of water. It looked so good that I decided to drink a little before I put the fish in it. I took a sip. The water was warm, so I put two ice cubes in it and went back upstairs. I dropped the fish into the glass and drained the bath. Then we went out for breakfast.

We went to a nice restaurant and ate waffles. I love

waffles. After that we went to the shop and bought another bowl. We brought it home and filled it with water.

"Go and get the fish," my mother said.

I went upstairs and brought the glass of water back down with me. The fish was swimming round and round the ice cubes.

My mother looked at the glass and said, "When did you put that fish in there?"

"Last night," I told her. "After I broke the bowl."

My mother shook her head and sighed. "You're lying," she said. "You couldn't have put the fish in that water last night. Where did it spend the night?"

It was time to tell the truth. It was time to tell the whole truth.

"In the bath, Mum," I said. "I'm sorry I lied. But how did you know that I put the fish in the glass this morning?"

How did she know?

6. THE SNAKE

Jessica Peters was driving Mary crazy. Every time Mary turned round, Jessica was there. Last week Jessica had come to school with Mary's haircut. The week before that, she had come to school in a dress exactly like Mary's. She had a jacket just like Mary's. Her hat was just the same as Mary's. And now, here she was with brand new shoes, just like Mary's. It was weird.

The Shadow, Mary thought. That's what she is. The Shadow.

The Shadow hung her jacket and hat on a hook at the back of the room. Then she moved away and waited.

Mary knew what she was waiting for. The Shadow was waiting to see where Mary was going to sit so that she could sit next to her.

Let her wait! Mary thought. The Shadow didn't really like her. In fact, she hardly knew her. She just wanted to be with her because she was suddenly popular. And why was she popular? Because Mary had become a soccer superstar. It wasn't because she was nice or anything. It was because she could run faster, and her right foot worked better than anybody else's in the school.

The Shadow wanted to be with her because she was the first girl to make the boys' soccer team.

But Mary couldn't think about that now. She had to think about her report. She had to think about Radar, the snake in the left pocket of her jacket. Some time today, Mary was going to have to tell her classmates all about that snake.

Luckily her jacket had zips on the pockets. She could just leave her snake in the pocket until it was time for her report. It was a blind snake, and blind snakes were used to hiding in dark places.

That's why they were blind.

Mary hung up her jacket and sat down. The Shadow sat next to her.

While Robert was giving his report, Mary folded her hands. The Shadow folded her hands, too. Mary put her hands in the pockets of her skirt. The Shadow did the same thing. It was very annoying.

At eleven o'clock the fire bell rang. Mary knew it wasn't really a fire. Whenever there was a drill, the bell rang at eleven o'clock.

Mary grabbed her jacket and raced to the front of the line. Then she looked around. Luckily, The Shadow was

too slow for her. She was way at the back, with the other slow people.

Mary couldn't wait to check to see if Radar was all right.

When they were outside, Mary shoved her hand inside the left pocket of her jacket. She wiggled her fingers around. She examined the lining of the pocket in case there was a hole. But there was no hole. And there was no snake. Radar was missing!

Mary's heart began to race. What had happened to her snake? She was sure that she had zipped up the pocket! Hadn't she? Maybe she had forgotten! Maybe Radar had wiggled out in the classroom. Maybe he was slithering around the desks right this minute, looking for insects! Maybe he was on the teacher's chair! Or maybe he'd even got into the teacher's drawer!

Mary shuddered. It was too awful to think about. How could she give her report without Radar? What if someone had taken him? What if someone had slid Radar into the teacher's bag?

Mary led the line back into the classroom. She hung up her jacket, and went back to her desk. When everyone was settled, the teacher called her name.

"We're ready for your report, Mary," she announced.

Mary rose slowly and shook her head. "I'm sorry," she said. "I can't give my report. I've lost my snake."

"You've *WHAT*!" the teacher cried.

"My snake's missing. It was in the pocket of my jacket, and now it's gone. I don't understand it. I'm sure I zipped up my pocket!"

"Well, look again!" the teacher said nervously.

Mary walked over to her jacket. She took it off the hook. She unzipped the pocket and slid her hand inside.

Something scaly brushed against her fingers. She touched it gently. Then she wrapped her fingers around it and pulled it out.

"But it wasn't there before!" she cried, as she held Radar up for everyone to see.

"Thank *goodness* you've found it!" the teacher said.

"*Really!* It really wasn't there before. Someone must have taken it and put it back." Mary swung around and glared at The Shadow.

"I don't think so," the teacher said. "I think your snake has been in that pocket all along."

How could that have happened?

7. THE PUDDLE

"**J**EREMY NORTH!**"** Jeremy's mother shouted from the kitchen.

Jeremy sighed and flicked off the telly. He knew that tone. He had forgotten something, and his mother was angry.

"JEREMY NORTH, YOU'VE FORGOTTEN THE RUBBISH AGAIN!

Jeremy skulked into the kitchen and went over to the bucket. He knew his mother was watching him, but he didn't look at her. He knew that she was scowling. She always scowled when he forgot one of his chores.

Jeremy carried the rubbish outside and dumped it into the bin. When he came back in, his mother was smiling.

"I have an idea," she said. "Let's go and see a film. There's a good one that starts in an hour. That gives me time to have a soak while you take the washing off the line. They say it's going to rain, so we'd better take it in."

Jeremy found the laundry basket and hurried outside. He liked films, especially on rainy days. He yanked the clothes off the line quickly and ran back inside. He could hear the bath water running above his head as he set the basket down on the kitchen table.

Jeremy sighed. His mother always took such a long time in the bath. He hoped they wouldn't be late for the film.

Jeremy went into the sitting room and turned the telly back on. Suddenly, thunder shook the room and rain pelted the windows. It was a good thing he had brought the laundry in. His mother wouldn't scowl at him today. He had done everything just right. Hadn't he?

"Quick, Jeremy!" his mother shouted from the top of the stairs. "Close all the windows before the rain gets in!" Jeremy turned off the telly and looked up at his mother. She hadn't changed her clothes yet. That meant she hadn't even taken her bath yet. Which meant that they were going to be late for the film.

He took his time closing the windows, but he was careful. He didn't want to get into trouble for not closing every single one. There were three windows in the sitting room, and he closed and locked each one of them. Then he closed and locked the kitchen door, and made sure that the kitchen window was shut tight. He checked all the windows one more time and sat down in front of the telly. The rain was rushing down the window panes, but Jeremy felt fine. He had done everything just right. There was no way that water would get into his house!

"Ready?" his mother asked from behind him.

Jeremy swung around and looked at her. She was still wearing the same clothes. "You haven't had your bath yet!"

"There isn't time," she said. "With all this rain, it will take us half an hour to get to the film. Did you shut the windows?"

"I sure did," Jeremy said proudly.

It was a long film, and Jeremy and his mother were hungry when they came out. It was still raining hard, so they decided to go straight home and have a snack

in their nice, dry kitchen.

But the kitchen wasn't dry at all! It was very, very wet! There was water everywhere; on the floor, on the table, on the counters.

"JEREMY NORTH!" Mrs North shouted.

"But Mum! I closed the windows! I closed the door! I did everything just right!"

"How could you have done everything right?" Mrs North cried angrily. "The room is flooded!"

Jeremy sloshed through the water and checked the window. It was locked up tight. Then he checked the door. No water could have got in there either.

He glanced around. There was no water in the sitting room, so it couldn't have come from there. Then where could it be coming from? This time he hadn't done anything wrong.

Had he? Had he?

Suddenly he remembered something, and he looked up at the ceiling. So that was it. He turned slowly and faced his mother. She was scowling down at him. He folded his arms and scowled right back. Because this time it was *her* fault.

What had his mother done?

8. THE RICH GIRL

The new girl was very, *very* rich. She lived in the biggest house on the street. Her family had the biggest car. And every day she wore wonderful, beautiful things to school. One day she wore a shiny necklace with a red jewel in it. The next day she wore fancy cowboy boots with golden toes. And the day after that she wore a watch that chimed and twinkled and played music every hour.

Some people even said she knew the Queen.

Her name was Annie Langdon. She sat alone in school and didn't talk to anyone. She went to fancy restaurants at dinnertime. And a man in a big red car picked her up right after school every day.

Lindy wanted to know her more than anything in the world. She wanted to be her friend. She wanted to go inside her great big house. She wanted to ride in her fancy car.

But it was very hard, because Annie wanted to be all

43

by herself.

Lindy thought about the new girl all the time. What was it like to be so rich? How did it feel to live in a house like that?

She wanted cowboy boots just like Annie's. She wanted a watch that played music every hour. She wanted a necklace with a red jewel.

She wanted to *be* Annie.

Lindy walked past Annie's big house twice every day. She passed it on the way *to* school. And she passed it on the way *from* school. Twice a day she stopped and looked up at the house. She wondered which room was Annie's. She wondered what her toys were like. She wondered if Annie had a bed covered with lace and silk.

Then, one day while she was standing there, she had an idea. She would just walk up to the door and knock. "Hello," she would say to the maid. "I'm Lindy. I'm Annie's cousin. I was kidnapped by wolves when I was a baby, and now I'm back. I've come to stay for a while."

And then she would stroll upstairs. She would go into one of the fancy bedrooms and go to sleep. The maid would wake her in the morning with tea and fancy cakes.

It was a fine plan. Lindy thought about it every day. She thought about it while she was having her breakfast. She thought about it while she was playing with her friends.

She thought about it when she was doing her chores.

Annie Langdon probably didn't have to do chores. Annie Langdon's maid probably did her chores for her.

And then, one day, Lindy did it. She just walked up to the door of Annie's grand house and rang the bell. The maid answered.

"Hello," Lindy said. "I'm Lindy. I'm Annie's cousin. I was kidnapped by wolves when I was a baby, and now I'm back. I've come to stay for a while."

She didn't wait for the maid to answer. She just pushed right by her and went up the big staircase. It was a fine staircase. It was all white and shiny and grand. Lindy strolled up it as if she lived there.

When she was at the top, she went into one of the bedrooms. There was lace everywhere. And velvet. Dark red velvet. Silver and gold necklaces lay on the tables. A lovely golden gown rested on the velvet chair.

Who lived in that room? Who wore those necklaces? Whose golden gown was it?

Lindy slid under the covers of the big bed and closed her eyes. In a minute someone would come in. But they wouldn't throw a sleepy little girl out into the cold. Would they?

But no one came. After a while Lindy fell asleep. When she woke up it was dark. She could hear footsteps in the hall. Music was playing somewhere. She climbed out of bed and tiptoed downstairs.

The long table was ready for supper. But no one was

sitting there. The candles were not lit. No one was drinking from the fancy glasses. No one was eating off the gold plates.

Lindy found some matches and lit the candles. Then she sat down and waited for the food to be brought in. She was not afraid, because she really believed that she belonged there now.

And then they came. Annie, and her mother and father, and lots of other people. It must have been a party.

"Hello Lindy," Annie said. "Is your room all right?"

"Fine," Lindy said. "Just fine."

"Who is this?" Annie's mother asked.

"It's Lindy, my kidnapped cousin. She's back." Annie winked at Lindy as she said this.

"But we don't have any kidnapped cousins," Mrs Langdon gasped.

"Yes we do," Annie said. "Tell her, Lindy."

Lindy was silent as the maid served the food. She didn't say anything when the maid brought in more food. She loved it there. She wanted to live there for ever. And Annie must have wanted her there, too.

Finally Lindy was ready to talk. "When I was a baby the wolves came," she said. "They took me out of my crib. They carried me through the night and set me down beside their babies. I grew up with the baby wolves. I did not see anyone but the wolves, ever. The wolves taught me to howl. They taught me how to catch my dinner. They taught me how to hide from all the bigger animals.

"And then, last year, I saw a person. He was camping by the lake. I had seen my face in the lake, and this man looked like me.

"He was the first person that I had seen since I was a baby, except for myself. He walked on two legs instead of four. I had never seen anyone do that before. I always walked on four legs, just like the wolves.

"Something strange happened when I saw that man. I

wanted to run to him. I wanted to talk to him. But all I could do was howl.

"The next day I wrote a note to the man and left it by the lake. I told him that I wanted to live with people instead of wolves. He brought me here to this town to live with his family.

"Now I want to come and live with my real family. I want to live with you."

Annie and her family were watching her carefully. They were thinking about what she had said. They were trying to decide if she was lying.

"You're not telling us the truth," Annie's mother said at last. "You couldn't have lived with the wolves since you were a baby. You knew how to do something that wolves don't know how to do. But maybe you can come and visit sometimes if your parents say it's all right."

What did Lindy know how to do?

9. MAKE ME HUMAN, TRUMAN

Timothy Truman wanted to be a cartoonist. He wanted to be a cartoonist more than anything in the world.

Every morning, before he went to school, he drew lines. He drew straight lines and curved lines. He drew squiggly lines. Before long the lines grew into trees and horses. Then, finally, the lines grew into people. Trees were easy. Animals and people were hard.

Timothy worked and worked. After a while, he could draw the face of a little girl. Sometimes the face was happy. Sometimes it was sad. And sometimes it was angry.

Timothy liked the face. It was nice.

Timothy thought about his cartoon all the time. He decided to call the face Monica. Monica the cartoon girl. That's what he would call her.

Monica would be a troublemaker. A nice troublemaker. And once in a while she would stamp her foot. I'll have to learn how to draw a foot, Timothy thought.

Monica the cartoon girl would have blonde hair. Her eyes would be blue and big. And she would have lots and lots of freckles.

Her little cartoon balloons would say things like, "I want to be human, Truman," and, "Make me swim, Tim."

Timothy spent most of his time with Monica. He made her laugh and jump and sleep and cry.

And then, one day, Timothy realised that Monica was perfect. She was the perfect little cartoon girl. Her ears were just right. Her hair was a perfect blonde colour. Her eyes were exactly right.

Timothy was ready to show her to someone. But who?

His family wouldn't care at all. They thought cartoons were silly. And most of his friends were too busy to care about Monica.

Timothy thought about it all week. And then, on Tuesday, he decided to show Monica to his art class. Timothy was late for art class that day. He had been so busy looking for just the right drawing that he had forgotten all about the time.

When he arrived the room was very quiet. Everyone was busy with their own drawings.

Timothy sat at a table in the corner. He placed his cartoon in front of him, face down. Then he leaned over and tapped Janet on the arm.

"What's going on?" he asked.

"We're drawing buildings," Janet said. "It's hard."

Timothy didn't think it was hard to draw a building. "You should try drawing a cartoon girl," he said. "*That's* hard."

But Janet was too busy drawing her building to care about what Timothy had to say.

Timothy glanced around the table. Everyone was drawing a different kind of building. Some were tall. Some were square. And one was even round.

There was one piece of paper and one marker left in the middle of the table. The marker was red.

"I guess I'll draw a red building," Timothy laughed.

"Everybody gets only one colour," Janet said. "So if you use red, your building will be red. We're supposed to pay attention to the lines, not the colours."

Timothy nodded and went to work. He worked for ten minutes, and then he stopped. He couldn't wait any longer. It was time to show someone his cartoon.

"Look at this!" he said to Janet.

"It's nice," Janet said. "But what does it mean?"

"What does what mean?"

"The words in the balloon above her head. What do you mean by 'Make me greater, creator'?"

"She's a cartoon girl who wants to be real," Timothy

said. "She has a mind of her own. Her name's Monica."

"Well, I like her," Janet said.

Timothy decided to pass the picture of Monica around the table.

"What do you think of this?" he said, as he passed the cartoon to his left. He was nervous. He was so nervous that he couldn't look as Monica went round the table.

After a while, his eyes shifted to the building on his right. The building was Janet's, and it was blue. He stared at it as she drew in four blue windows. He watched her carefully, and soon he began to forget about Monica.

His gaze stayed on Janet's blue building the whole time that Monica was moving around the table.

Janet kept working on her blue building until the cartoon reached her.

And then he saw it. His drawing of Monica had gone around the circle. Now it was being passed to Janet. In a minute he would have to look up and hear what they thought of his picture.

The paper was face down, but he knew it was his cartoon.

He turned to his left and looked away from Janet. He did not want to see her looking at his drawing. He knew she was still drawing. He could hear her.

Why isn't she looking at Monica? he wondered.

Suddenly, Janet poked him, hard. Timothy swung

around and faced her.

"It's *really* nice," she said. "I think 'Make me greater, creator,' is funny."

Timothy smiled and looked down at his cartoon.

Something was wrong.

Something was very wrong.

Something was very, very wrong with Monica. Monica's hair was GREEN!

Timothy gasped and stood up. He stood up so fast that his chair tipped over.

GREEN HAIR? Monica didn't have green hair! She had blonde hair! Timothy loved her blonde hair. Who could have done this?

Timothy studied the hands of the artists around the table. Everyone was still clutching the markers that they had been clutching before.

But no one was clutching a green one.

Timothy read the words one more time. "Make me greater, creator."

Someone at that table must have thought that "greater" meant green hair.

But who?

Timothy closed his eyes and thought for a minute. And then he knew.

Do you?

10. THE FLASHING LIGHT

"**H**e's in trouble!" Damon cried.

Damon sounded scared, but I didn't know what to do.

Damon is my best friend. He lives across the street from me, and we're together all the time. I help him, and he helps me. But this time I didn't think I could do anything at all.

"A flashing light woke me last night," he said. "It was shining right into my eyes. I jumped out of bed and went to the window, and there it was. It was very, very dark outside, so all I could see was the light. It must have been far away, but it was hard to tell.

The light flashed three times, fast. Then it flashed three long flashes, then three short ones. It did it again, and again, and again. Three short, three long, three short. That's the SOS signal, Mary! That guy with the torch must have been in trouble!"

"Well," I said. "Did you get help?"

He said he hadn't. He said he didn't think anybody would believe him.

I knew what he was talking about. Some people think that Damon's a liar. But I know better. He just has an active imagination. He likes to make up stories.

He says he wants to be a writer when he grows up, which seems about right.

I didn't know if he was telling the truth or not.

The next day he said he saw the light again. "It was closer this time," he said. "He was flashing the same SOS signal, over and over again. He must be in big trouble. Maybe he's moving towards us."

I didn't sleep at all that night. I sat by my window and waited to see the light. I was worried about the person with the torch. What could have happened to him? Maybe he had been washed ashore on a huge tidal wave. Maybe he had fallen out of a plane. Maybe he had escaped from an animal trap.

The clock by my bed read 3:00am when I finally saw the light. It was coming from somewhere across the street.

At first I thought it was in Damon's window. But it wasn't. It was near his house, though. It was right next to his house.

I didn't know what to do. Maybe it was Damon. Maybe he was trying to scare me.

Or maybe it was someone signalling for our help.

I should have told my parents, but I didn't. I was silly. I got dressed and tiptoed downstairs. When I was outside, I raced across the street.

I was searching for the light when I heard something. It was a noise in the bushes beside Damon's house.

I dived into the bushes without thinking. If I had thought about it I probably wouldn't have done it. You can get hurt doing things like that.

But I did it. I dived.

Somebody was there. I felt his hair. I felt his jacket. I felt the torch.

"Who are you?" I shouted. Boy, was I scared!

The person in the bushes flashed the light, and I saw who it was. It was Damon.

"Damon!" I said. "You're a liar! You were flashing that light!"

"No, I wasn't," Damon said. "I saw the light and came out here. I couldn't find the person, but I found this red torch in the bushes. He must have dropped it here."

Damon showed me the torch. Then we looked around for a while, but there was no sign of the person.

As I was walking home I remembered something. Damon had made up that whole story. He had known too much. He had given himself away.

I decided never, *ever* to believe him again.

How did Damon give himself away?

11. THE VULTURE

"**D**on't touch the vulture!" my aunt told me, as I was climbing into bed.

I had no intention of touching that vulture! Ever! I didn't even want to look at it, but I had no choice. The huge black bird was hanging right above my head!

My aunt said good night. She said that it was nice that I was visiting. Then she went across the room and opened the window a little bit so that I would have some air.

I pulled the covers over my head so that I wouldn't have to see the vulture. I mumbled good night, but I don't think she heard me.

When she was gone, I slid the covers down and peered into the darkness. After a while, I began to make out shadows around the room. I could see the black outline of my suitcase, and I wished that I had never come here.

One whole week of sleeping under that horrible, creepy vulture! I would have a heart attack for certain!

And that was just what that slimy creature wanted me to do! Wasn't it?

But Aunt Anne had said not to touch it. Hadn't she?

I closed my eyes and tried to sleep, but I could feel it up there, waiting. I opened my eyes and looked up. The dark shadow above my head was moving. The wind that was blowing through the open window was making it bob up and down.

Suddenly, as I watched, the vulture's head swung round, and dipped downwards. Those eyes! Horrible, round bright yellow eyes! They were staring right at me, as if they were waiting for something!

I was being silly. The vulture wasn't even real. It was just a big piece of wool that my aunt had sewed and stuffed with cotton when she was younger. But it was still frightening. And those eyes! Those awful yellow eyes!

I pulled the covers over my head again and tried to sleep. The wind was blowing harder now, and I could hear the vulture banging against the wall above my head. *THUMP! THUMP! THUMP!* Over and over.

I knew the yellow eyes were watching me. As I slipped into a restless sleep, I wondered if it was waiting for me. I wondered if it was waiting until ... I wondered ... I wondered...

I must have slept for about an hour, because I was very tired the next morning. One more night with that vulture, and I'd definitely have a heart attack. I had to do *something*! But what?

I thought about it all day long. I thought about it at the lake, and while I was having my dinner, and while I was watching the telly.

"Aunt Anne?" I said, as I was going upstairs.

"Yes dear?"

"Could you take the vulture down? Maybe you could put it away until I'm gone."

"Don't be silly, dear," Aunt Anne said. "It's just a stuffed bird. You used to have lots of stuffed animals."

"Then maybe I could sleep in another room," I pleaded.

But it was no use. My aunt just shook her head and said, "You're much too old to be frightened by something like that."

Ha! I thought. I was *terrified*.

I went upstairs and closed the door to my room. I looked up at the horrible black thing, and I made a decision. I was not going to sleep in the same room as that vulture. It was him or me. I would get rid of it.

I climbed on my bed and reached up. The shiny yellow eyes watched me as I yanked the string that held it to the ceiling. They glared at me as I carried it to the window. They stared up at me as I dangled it above the ground.

When it was gone, I went into the shower and turned on the water, *hard*. I stayed there for a long time, and then I dried myself, put on my pyjamas, and went into my room.

My aunt was sitting on my bed. She didn't say a word. She just waited, like the vulture.

"Where is it?" she said after a long time.

"What?"

"The bird, of course. What did you do with it?" Bird? Bird? That wasn't a bird. It was a hungry, horrible vulture!

I thought quickly, and then I said, "It was hanging up there when I went into the shower."

"Really?" Aunt Anne sighed.

"Yes! Yes!" I insisted. "And while I was in the shower I heard it!"

"Oh really?" Aunt Anne said again. She looked like she believed me, so I continued, talking faster.

"It must have been frightened of me, lying there right below it all night long. Yes, that's right. Those yellow eyes looked really scared of me. And while I was taking a shower, I heard it flap its wings and sail over to the window. I heard it thump down on to the grass. It took its time. I heard the whole thing."

"I don't think so," my aunt said.

"Why not?" I was really curious. It sounded like a good story to me.

"Because you couldn't possibly have heard it."

Why not?

12. THE CASE OF THE JUNK FOOD THIEF

Lydia O'Neal lived in the old house up on the hill. She was only ten years old, but she lived there all alone, and she was just fine.

Lydia had been living by herself for a month now, and she liked it. She didn't choose it. It just happened. One day she had gone out for a long, long bike ride, and she had got lost. It took her five days to get back home, and by then her family had moved.

"I guess they didn't like it here without me," Lydia said to herself. At first she was sad, but then she liked the idea of being there alone.

Her family and friends had searched outside the house, but they couldn't find her. They had looked inside while she was gone, so they didn't bother to search it again.

Lydia loved living in the big house alone. She didn't tell anyone that she had returned. She just stayed and stayed, until everyone forgot about her.

Finally she ran out of food, so she called her friend Omar. She could trust Omar. He wouldn't tell anyone she was there.

"Hello Omar," she said, when he answered the phone.

"Where *are* you?" Omar cried. "I thought you were gone for ever."

"I'm here. At home. But don't tell. I like it here by myself."

Omar promised not to tell. He also promised to come by the next morning. Lydia needed food.

That night Lydia decided to change the house. It was *her* house now. She moved the chairs around and made a place to dance. She put the telly right in the middle of the sitting room. She hung sheets over the windows so that no one could see in.

And then she decided to paint.

She found a big can of red paint in the basement and went to work. First she painted the fridge red. Next she painted one wall in the sitting room red. Then she took off the doorknob and painted the front door red. Not the part of the door that faced outside. Just the part you could see from inside the house.

Lydia didn't want anyone to know she was in there.

She was still painting when Omar arrived the next morning.

"Watch the paint!" she shouted, as Omar came in.

Omar looked around and groaned. "Red?" he sighed.

"RED? What will your parents say?" Omar wasn't really a lot of fun.

Lydia gave him a wad of money and smiled sweetly. "My parents are gone," she said. "It's my house now. Here's some money that I found in my mother's desk. Will you go to the shop and buy me some crisps and some biscuits and some sweets and some pudding?"

"Crisps!" Omar cried. "Sweets! Pudding! What about apples and lettuce? What about milk and bananas?" Lydia had forgotten that Omar didn't eat any junk food. He wasn't allowed to eat it. He wasn't even allowed to *look* at it.

"Just go, Omar," Lydia said. "Just get the food."

Omar shook his head in disgust and grabbed the open door. He pulled it shut angrily and ran to the shop. He was back in half an hour.

Lydia met him on the forecourt. "Quick!" she cried. "Give me the food. I'm starving!"

Omar handed her the bag and watched as she opened it.

"What's *THIS*?" she shouted, as she looked in the bag.

"What's what?"

"Someone has eaten all my food! The crisp bag is empty. The biscuit packet is empty. The soda bottle is empty. And the sweets are gone. You ate all my food, Omar!"

"It wasn't me," Omar insisted. "I'm not allowed to eat those things."

"Then who was it?"

Omar thought for a minute. "It must have been the dog," he said at last.

"What dog?"

"I put the bag down for a minute and a big dog came over. He sniffed the bag. I guess he ate the food."

"That's silly, Omar," Lydia said. "Dogs can't open soda bottles. What are all these red marks on the packets?"

Omar had to think about that for a long time. But he had an answer. "The dog had a cut on his nose. It must be dog blood."

"*You* ate my food, Omar," Lydia announced. "And if you hold out your hand I can prove it. You should be ashamed of yourself. Eating junk food, and so early in the morning, too!"

What was on Omar's hand?

13. THE TRIPLETS

Mr Browne's Junk Shop was filled with wonder. It had everything. A scratched and faded table overflowed with old Hallowe'en costumes. Music boxes tinkled. Ballerinas danced throughout the dusty room. And kites floated from the ceiling.

The Martin triplets loved Mr Browne's Junk Shop more than any other shop in town. They came every day at three, because it was on their way home from school. Day after day, they searched through the boxes for new treasures; marbles, books, dolls, old jewellery, anything.

On this day they found something so special that it made Amanda Martin cry out, "What is it?"

"It's an old photo machine," Mr Browne explained. "Go behind the curtain. Put some coins in. Then push the button. The machine takes a picture of *you*. Before you know it, your picture comes out of the slot."

The Martin triplets raced over to the machine and sat

on the seat in front of the camera. Amanda dropped in some coins and folded her arms. Sally wanted to get one picture of each of them, alone. But the others thought that was a terrible idea.

"Nobody can tell us apart anyway," Amanda said. "So let's take pictures of the three of us being silly."

"Of course they can tell us apart," Sally groaned. "Ever since you and Jane had your hair cut and I didn't, we've been different."

Sally was tired of looking different. It was more fun being the same. Three pictures together might be more fun, too. "All right," she said. "Three silly pictures it is."

When the pictures came out of the slot, they were very silly indeed. In the first picture, they all had their tongues out. In the second, they were pretending to be monkeys. And in the third they looked like they were sound asleep.

"Can you tell who is who?" Sally asked Mr Browne when they came out.

Mr Browne studied the picture and shook his head. "Well, it's easy to pick you out, Sally, with the long hair," he laughed. "But your sisters are a lot harder."

Sally noticed the helmet when she was almost to the door. Her sisters were already outside, but the helmet was so wonderful that it made her stop. It was covered with red and blue buttons and large silver knobs. An antenna rose from the top.

Sally lifted it from the box and slipped it onto her head. She turned a knob and waited. In seconds the inside of the helmet came alive with pictures of racing horses. She pushed a red button. Music filled the inside

of the helmet as the horses moved in front of her eyes.

"How much is it worth?" she shouted, as she pulled the helmet from her head.

"Ten pounds," Mr Browne said. "It's very special."

It was too special for Sally. She would never have ten pounds. She sighed and placed it back in the box, gently. In an hour, the triplets were back in Mr Browne's Junk Shop.

"My, my," Mr Browne laughed. "Now I'll never be able to tell you apart. You sound alike, and now you all *look* exactly alike."

"I didn't like looking different from my sisters," Sally said, as she followed Amanda and Jane to the back.

They stayed in the photo booth for several minutes. When they came out, Amanda and Jane went straight to the door. But Sally stayed behind, to touch her helmet. She stroked it gently, then lifted it from the box.

She wanted that helmet more than anything in the whole world. She wanted it so badly that she thought about taking it.

But Mr Browne was staring at her. He was watching her so carefully that it made her nervous. She shuffled her feet. She shrugged her shoulders. She brushed some hair off of her dark blue jersey.

How will he ever know it was me? Sally thought. We all look alike now, so maybe he'll think I'm Amanda or Jane. He'll never, ever be able to prove which one of us took it. Will he?

Sally slipped the helmet onto her head and left the shop. Mr Browne was right behind her, just as she knew he would be. She began to run. She raced around the corner, and skidded to a stop in an alley. She hid the helmet quickly and began to run again.

Her sisters were waiting for her at the next corner. And so was Mr Browne.

"I took a short cut, Sally," he explained.

"I'm not Sally," Sally said.

"Yes you are. And I can prove it." He pulled a strip of photos out of his pocket. "You dropped these. These are the pictures you took the second time. After you went to get your hair cut. Look at your shoulders."

Sally stared at the photos. "We look exactly alike," she whined. And they did look alike. They were wearing the same clothes. They had the same faces. And now they had the same haircuts. There was no way at all to tell them apart. Or was there?

Mr Browne pointed to Sally's shoulders. There was something covering her blue jersey that gave her away.

Do you know what it was?

14. THE THING UNDER THE TRAP DOOR

The building had been empty for a long, long time. No one lived there. There were no lights in the building. And no one went into the building, so no one knew if there were sounds inside.

"I wonder when they'll knock it down," Enzo said one day. He was standing in front of the building with his best friend Jake.

"Never," Jake answered. "I think they'll fix it up and rich people will buy all the flats. Maybe my parents will buy a flat."

"Your parents aren't rich," Enzo reminded him.

"Well then, maybe I'll just live there myself. Maybe I'll go inside and settle in right now." Jake straightened his shoulders and walked towards the building.

Enzo couldn't believe it. Jake wanted to go into that creepy, scary building that no one ever went into!

"Well? Are you coming or not?" Jake asked impatiently.

"I guess so," Enzo said. He did *not* want to go into that building. But he couldn't let his best friend go in there alone. Could he?

Jake and Enzo walked up the path and stopped at the building. Enzo glanced up at the big windows. It was beginning to get dark. If they were going to explore the inside of the building, they'd have to hurry.

Jake walked towards some stone steps that led down to a little open door, then changed his mind.

"Come on," he said, as he raced up the steps and opened the main door.

Strange shadows danced on the walls as they made their way down the main hallway. Jake led the way, stopping at each doorway. When they reached the last room, they went back to the room in the front of the building. They went inside.

It was a huge room with high ceilings. In one corner

there was a large fireplace with a log in the grate.
"*Jake!*" Enzo cried. "*Look!*"

Jake came over and looked. Enzo was pointing to the
floor beside the fireplace.

"What is it?" Jake whispered.

"It's a trap door."

"I *know* that. But what do you think it's for?"

Enzo knelt down and tried to open it, but it wouldn't
budge. "Maybe they kept the firewood down there," he
suggested.

"Or maybe there's something else down there," Jake
said. "Like hidden treasure. Or a wild animal. Maybe a
lion or an animal with horns and huge teeth lives there."

Enzo stood up and shivered. It was really getting dark
now. The shadows had deepened. In a few minutes it
would be pitch dark, and they wouldn't be able to see
anything.

Enzo and Jake did not speak for a long, long time. They just stood there and thought about the thing under the trap door. Then, when it was too dark to see anything at all, Enzo said, "I wonder if it ever comes out."

Jake did not answer. Enzo peered through the darkness, but he couldn't see his friend.

Suddenly, a soft scratching sound came from under the trap door.

Scratch, scratch, scratch.

Enzo froze. He was so terrified that he could not speak. He could not move. He could not do anything except stand there and wait.

The thing stopped scratching. For a while it was silent. And then it began to bang. It banged the underside of the door loudly.

Bang, bang, bang.

It was too dark for Enzo to see the trap door now, but he knew that it was still closed. He could tell by the sound of the banging.

Suddenly, the banging stopped. The room was dead quiet. Still, Enzo could not move. He stood there, alone in the room, frozen, waiting.

And then the trap door squeaked. The thing was pushing the door from underneath. The thing was coming out. The door squeaked again, then again and again as the thing pushed it slowly, slowly upward.

Enzo couldn't breathe. His body went cold. He was terrified. "Jake?" he whispered.

"Yes?" Jake replied.

What was the thing ? How did it get there?

15. UP IN SMOKE

Jeremy Dunn parked his bike in front of Mr Woodward's sweet shop and went inside. Mr Woodward was flipping through a notebook.

"Well hello, Jeremy," Mr Woodward said. "I've just been thinking about you."

"You have?"

Mr Woodward pointed to a page in the notebook. "I've been thinking that you owe me five pounds, Jeremy. Every day you buy sweets. Every day you have no money. Every day you promise to pay the next day. And every day I write it down in my book."

Jeremy sighed. Five pounds! Where would he get five pounds?

"I'll be back," he promised Mr Woodward.

That night, Jeremy went through his drawers. Then he went through his pockets and his wallet. When he was finished, he had five pounds in coins. Five pounds exactly. No more and no less.

There were too many coins to carry, so he put them into a small metal box with a cover.

The next morning he took the box to Mr Woodward's Sweet Shop. As he rode his bike around the corner, a wall of black smoke greeted him.

"*Oh No!*" Jeremy cried when he saw that it was Mr Woodward's shop that was on fire.

Mr Woodward was standing near a fire engine and he was crying.

"I'm sorry," Jeremy whispered, but Mr Woodward didn't hear him.

Jeremy watched the firemen put out the fire, and then he went home for dinner. As he ate he thought about the metal box filled with coins. Mr Woodward would really need money now.

Jeremy ate his dinner quickly and went back to the shop with the money. The firemen were still there, but Mr Woodward had gone.

Jeremy looked inside. The shop was dark and wet and it smelled of smoke. He stepped back.

He knew that he shouldn't go inside. He knew that it was probably dangerous. Maybe he'd wait a while.

Jeremy stared into the gloomy shop and thought about the money. Mr Woodward probably had lots of insurance. He might even make money out of this fire. But he, Jeremy, was broke. Or at least he would be after he gave all his money to Mr Woodward.

Suddenly, Jeremy had a brilliant idea. He would *pretend* to return the money, but he wouldn't really do it. He jumped on his bike and raced back home.

An hour later he was back. He was carrying the metal box, but now the box had a note taped onto it. The note said, "Dear Mr Woodward. Here is the five pounds that I owe you. Thank you. Jeremy Dunn."

The firemen were gone now, and Mr Woodward was nowhere around.

Jeremy tiptoed into the charred building and looked around. The place was a mess.

The sweet jars lay melted on the floor. The shelves were gone. The only thing left of Mr Woodward's rocking chair was a burned leg.

For a moment Jeremy wondered if he was doing the right thing. Mr Woodward had been so kind to him. But Mr Woodward would be rich now, and Jeremy would be very poor if he gave away all his money.

Jeremy opened the top of the metal box. The box was empty. The coins were back where they belonged, in his top drawer. Then he closed the top and tossed the box on to what was left of the counter.

Jeremy was very proud of himself. He had never made up such a clever plan before. He would tell Mr Woodward that he had returned the money. He would say that he had put a five pound note inside the box.

"I put the metal box on the counter before the fire," he would say. "And the five pound note must have burned up."

But that would be impossible if the lid was closed. Jeremy opened the lid and started to leave the shop.

But then he had another idea. Maybe he should make it look like the five pound note had fallen out of the box. It if had been *inside* the box, it might not have burned.

Jeremy knocked the box onto the floor. It landed face down.

The next day, after school, Jeremy stopped by the shop. Mr Woodward was inside. He was picking through the charred wood.

"I'm really sorry about the fire," Jeremy said.

"Thank you," Mr Woodward replied sadly. "But I guess I'll be all right. Luckily, I had insurance."

Jeremy felt better. He would have felt terrible if Mr Woodward was broke. "Did you find my five pounds?" Jeremy asked.

Mr Woodward said that he hadn't.

"I left it in a metal box.".

"When was that?" Mr Woodward asked.

"Yesterday morning."

Mr Woodward glanced around the room. "Before the

fire then," he said. "There can't be much left of it. Everything that can burn has burned to a crisp. But wait. You said it was in a metal box?"

Jeremy pointed to the floor. "There it is," he said. "See. Over there, with the note on it. Wait a minute. It looks like the top is open. Maybe the money fell out and burned."

"Maybe," Mr Woodward muttered. He walked over to the box and picked it up. He turned it round and round, and then he looked up at Jeremy.

"No five pound note here," he said.

"Guess it burned," Jeremy sighed.

"I don't think so," Mr Woodward told him. "This box wasn't in the fire at all. You're lying."

Jeremy took a deep breath and frowned.

"You still owe me five pounds, Jeremy Dunn!" Mr Woodward said angrily. "And I can prove it!"

How did Mr Woodward know that Jeremy put the box in the shop AFTER the fire, and not before?

16. THE MONSTER IN THE BATH

When my little brother Robert screamed, I laughed so hard that I fell off my chair.

I knew why he was screaming, of course. But nobody else did. We were all having our dinner. Well, almost all of us. Robert was upstairs taking a bath, so he wasn't there.

Robert was still screaming when he came downstairs. He was shaking his arms and screaming and screaming. He still had his clothes on, so he must have seen the monster before he turned on the water.

"A *monster!*" he hollered. "There's a *monster* in the bath!"

I couldn't stop laughing, so he knew I had done it.

"You put it there!" Robert screamed. "It was you! It was you! I'll never take a bath again."

"What's this about a monster, Ellie?" Mum asked.

I stopped laughing and said, "Oh, Robert's just seeing things again. There's no monster in the bath."

"Well, go and take your bath then, Robert," Mum told him.

Robert started to cry and scream again. "Never!" he shouted. "I will never, ever, take a bath again in my life!"

"All right, dear," Mum said. "Then eat your dinner." I guess she thought he'd get over it soon.

"Ellie put it there!" Robert announced. "She put it there and I'm going to prove it!"

"Yes dear," my Mum said, smiling.

"Aren't you even going to *look* at the monster?" Robert pleaded.

So Mum and Dad and I followed Robert upstairs. We went into the bathroom and waited for him to show us the monster.

"There!" Robert said, as he pointed to the front of the bath. "See. The hot and cold taps look just like monster eyes. And look at the spout where the water comes out. It's a long horrible nose. It's like some creepy monster is sneezing water at me. Yuchh!"

It was true. It *did* look like a terrible monster. The taps and spout were part of a monster face.

I had done a *great* job!

"Ellie did it!" Robert shouted. "She drew it there with a marker. I know she did it, and I am going to prove it!"

Sometimes Robert is a little detective.

My parents thought the monster was funny. They

didn't mind at all.

"Very clever," my Dad said.

Robert went crazy after that. He lay on his bed all the time. All he thought about was the monster in the bathtub. All he talked about was the monster in the bathtub. And he refused to take a bath.

"I'm busy," he said when my Mum told him he was looking dirty.

"You don't look busy to me. You've been lying on your bed all day."

"I'm thinking," Robert said. "I'm thinking about the monster. I have to prove that Ellie did it.".

"Of course she did it, Robert," my Mum said. "We all know that."

"I have to prove it," Robert sighed.

Robert got dirtier and dirtier. His hair started caking. His fingernails turned black. But he wouldn't take a bath.

"All right, Robert," I said after four days. "I've washed off the monster. It's gone. Now go take a bath. *Please!*"

"I'm busy thinking," Robert said.

As I said, Robert is a little detective sometimes. Then, on the fifth day, he stopped thinking.

"I *have* it!" he said.

"You have what?" my Dad asked.

"I can prove that Ellie drew the monster."

"Oh good," my Dad groaned. "Does that mean you can take a bath now?"

"Maybe. But Ellie has to say she did it first."

I sighed and said I did it. "Will you take a bath now?" I asked.

"Not until I prove it," Robert said. "All right. I've been thinking about the day the monster appeared. First it wasn't there. And then it was. I went into the bathroom at five o'clock. The bathtub was empty. There was no monster. I went downstairs. Mum and Dad were in the kitchen, cooking dinner. I helped them cook. Mum left the kitchen once, at a quarter past five. Dad left the kitchen once, at half past five. I went up to take a bath at seven, while the dinner was in the oven. The bathtub was full of very hot water. The monster was there."

"I made it when I was in the bath," I said.

"At first I thought Mum had done it," Robert said, ignoring me. "But she was in the kitchen. Then I thought it was Dad. But he was in the kitchen too. The culprit must have been in the bath when they drew it."

"I *did* it, Robert," I groaned.

"*Now* I can prove that Ellie was the *only* person who could have done it. Something wet gave her away."

Do you know what it was?

17. JAMIE'S STORY

Jamie jumped on my head at seven o'clock this morning and scared me to death. Jamie is my little brother. He's six. I've told him not to jump on my head when I'm sleeping, but he won't listen. This morning he jumped on me really hard. He wanted me to get up and listen.

I told him to go away but he wouldn't. So I listened. First he asked if I had heard the storm. I said, "Sure I did. The thunder was crashing all night. The lightning kept waking me up. Why?"

"Why?" he asked. "*Why?* Because I was outside in the storm all night. I was lost all night. I couldn't sleep at all, so I went for a walk. I just kept walking and walking, until I was up in the mountains. Suddenly it started to rain. It started to thunder and there was lightning. The wind took me off my feet. It carried me to the edge of a cliff. It picked me up and tossed me over the cliff. I fell all the way down the mountain and landed in some bushes. I lay there for a long time and listened to the storm. I didn't cry or scream, because I'm brave."

"After a while I heard some funny noises. I turned and looked around me. It was very dark, but I could make out some shadows. I saw three shadowy kittens behind a big rock, and I went to them. We sat in the dark together and listened to the thunder and the wind."

"All of a sudden I heard a loud growl. I looked up quickly and saw two bright eyes shining from the cliff above me. The thing growled again."

"Lightning shot through the sky, and lit up the thing. The eyes belonged to a huge lioness. I waited for the next lightning bolt. When it came, I saw that the kittens were lion cubs.."

"The mother lion growled again and leapt off the cliff. She sailed through the air towards her cubs. And towards me."

"I rolled through the bushes and raced through the mud. The lioness was right behind me. I could feel her breath on my neck. I dived into a cave and quickly hid in a corner. The lioness followed, then went back to her cubs."

"I stayed in the cave all night long. Outside, the rain came down and thunder rattled the sky."

"Ten wild dogs came into the cave. I hid in the corner, so that they couldn't see me. I could hear them sniffing and searching, but I was too smart for them. I found a little nook and sqeezed myself in. Three of the dogs sniffed around the nook. I could feel them breathing near me, but I didn't move. I hardly breathed."

"After a while they went away."

"When it was light, I wandered out. The rain was still coming down, but the thunder had stopped. Every time I stepped down, mud covered my feet. It squished

between my toes and slid down my ankles."

"I trudged home. It was very hard in the mud. But I finally made it, and here I am. Aren't you glad to see me?"

"Sure I am," I said. "But why aren't you wet?"

"I changed my clothes before I came into your room," Jamie explained. "I left my shoes outside, and went straight into the bathroom. I took a bath and threw my clothes in the laundry."

"Wait a minute!" I said. "Say that again!"

He said it again and grinned.

Something was wrong with his story. And then I remembered.

Jamie was lying. He hadn't been out in the storm at all. "Your shoes aren't outside!" I said. "You weren't wearing any shoes. The mud squished through your toes. Remember?"

"Oh," Jamie whispered. "Well, then. What I meant to say was that I came straight into the house and walked up to the bathroom."

"Through the kitchen?" I asked.

"That's right."

I jumped out of bed and told him to follow me. "We'll have a look at the kitchen, then," I said. "Come on."

But when we went into the kitchen, something was missing. If Jamie had *really* been out in the storm, they would have been there.

What was missing?

18. THE PLANT DID IT

Mrs Jones knocked on the front door at noon. I was watching the telly all by myself because the rest of the family was out in the garden.

"Hello, Mrs Jones," I said. "How are you?".

"Fine, Raymond," she said. "I'm going on a trip and I need your help."

"You do?"

"Yes. I need you to water my plant while I'm away. And don't forget to bring in the newspaper, too."

I wanted to ask how much she was going to pay me, but I didn't. I knew that wouldn't be a nice thing to say, so I just waited for her to tell me.

She smiled and told me that she would be leaving that night. Then she gave me the key to her house.

But she didn't say a word about money.

I thought about it when she was gone. Mrs Jones was a nice lady and I knew she would pay me when she came back.

I went over to her house the next day and unlocked the door. I placed the newspaper on the floor in the hallway and looked around. There was only one plant in the house, but it was big. *Very* big. That plant would need lots of glasses of water if it was going to live until Mrs Jones came back.

I found a big glass and filled it with lots of water. Then I carried the water back into the hallway and dumped it into the plant-pot.

The plant made a strange noise as it slurped up the water.

I jumped back and waited, but the plant didn't make any more noise. It just sat there on the shelf and waited.

I was about to go back into the kitchen for more water when I noticed the tiny statue. It was on a shelf next to the plant. I picked it up gently and looked it over.

The statue was a tiny king. He was wearing beautiful robes made of tiny little pieces of coloured glass. Golden threads were woven through the red and blue and yellow robes.

Maybe I will buy a wonderful king like that when Mrs Jones gives me my money, I thought.

I put the king back onto the shelf carefully and looked over at the plant.

It was still waiting.

I gave it another glass of water, then another and

another. Every time I poured the water into its soil, it made that same strange noise.

"AHHHHHHH!" it said.

The day after that was Monday. I stopped by Mrs Jones' house on my way to school. I placed the newspaper on top of the one from the day before, and then I felt the plant. It was thirsty and dry again, so this time I gave it seven glasses of water.

I was about to leave when I noticed that the little glass king was watching me. His eyes seemed frightened. I went back to the shelf and took him down. Those tiny frightened eyes seemed to follow me as I moved him around. In a way he seemed real.

I knew that was silly, so I put him back on the shelf and went to school. I didn't think about the king at all that day. And I didn't think about the plant either.

The next morning I was late for school. I tossed the paper onto the pile and hurried over to the shelf. That was when I noticed something very strange.

The plant was growing. Its leaves were creeping all over the place.

The frightened eyes of the tiny glass king watched me as I gave the plant ten glasses of water.

The next day the plant was even bigger. I was early that day, and I took my time picking up the newspaper.

I read it for a little while, and then I dropped it onto the pile.

And then I glanced up at the plant. It was too big for the shelf now, so I took it down and put it on the floor. I gave it lots and lots and *lots* of water this time, because it was *very* thirsty.

"*AHH*," it said. "*AHHHHHHHHHHHH.*"

When I was finished, I went over to the little king. His eyes didn't seem frightened any more. They seemed happy now. I wondered how much a little king like that would cost. I wondered how much money Mrs Jones was going to give me.

The plant was much bigger the next day. The leaves were creeping up the wall and around the shelf. The little king watched me as I gave it water. His eyes were frightened again. But there was something else. They seemed to be pleading with me.

Did the little king want me to do something?

I thought about the little king all night long. I wondered why it was so frightened. I wondered if it knew something that I didn't know.

Mrs Jones would be home the next day. I was sure she would be happy that her plant had grown so much. But what would she think about her sad little king?

Maybe she won't pay me if the little king is sad, I thought. Maybe she won't like me any more.

I woke up very early the next day and went over to her house. My plan was to make the little king happy. But when I got there I couldn't find the little king at all.

At first I didn't look for him. As usual, I placed the newspaper on top of the pile of papers in the hallway. Then I checked the plant. It was very dry and thirsty.

I was about to go into the kitchen when I noticed the little king. He was watching me with the saddest eyes I've ever seen.

And then I saw why. The leaves of the plant were all around him, like arms. During the night they had grown higher and higher. Now they were hugging him, tighter and tighter.

As I watched, the arms grew bigger and bigger and

bigger, until I couldn't see the little king at all any more.

Even his sad, frightened eyes were hidden by those huge green arms.

"*NO!*" I screamed, as I raced to the shelf and ripped the arms out of the way.

"*AHHHHHH!*" groaned the plant, as I grabbed the little king and ripped it free.

Suddenly, one of the arms brushed my cheek and scared me to death. I raised my hand to brush it away, and as I did so I dropped the little king.

I couldn't believe it! The little king floated slowly towards the floor, watching me the whole way. He seemed to be frowning as he fell. I thought I saw a tiny tear fall from his sad eyes.

I tried to catch him, but I was too late. The little king hit the floor and shattered into hundreds of pieces.

I sat on the floor and cried, and then I ran out of there. I felt terrible all day. Later that day, when Mrs Jones knocked on my door, I was still feeling terrible.

"Hello, Raymond," she said.

"Hello," I whispered.

"My plant is very big," she said. "You must have given it lots of water."

"It was very thirsty."

"Yes. Well, I was wondering what had happened to the little king. It seems to be broken."

"Oh?" I said. "Is it really?"

"Yes, Raymond. It's all over the floor."

I frowned and tried to look puzzled. "Well, the plant must have done it, then," I said. "I wasn't there at all today. I decided the plant had enough water."

"Are you sure you didn't come over today?" Mrs Jones asked.

"I'm very sure," I said.

"You're lying, Raymond," Mrs Jones said. "And I can prove it. I don't like liars, Raymond. I'm so sorry about the little king. I was going to give it to you for watering the plant, Raymond. And now I don't have anything to give you. What a shame, Raymond. What a shame."

How could Mrs Jones prove that Raymond had been there that day?

19. FOOTSTEPS

"Oh all right!" Janie sighed. "I'll take you to the zoo. But then we're going to the beach. And you have to promise to leave me alone when we get there."

"I promise," Toni said.

Janie was a teenager, and she was always sighing. And she always wanted to be by herself. But she couldn't be, because she had to take care of Toni.

Toni hated it. She hated being the little sister. She hated being in the way. She hated Janie sighing at her all the time.

But there was nothing that she could do about it. Toni ran outside and looked up at the sun. It was going to be a fine day for the zoo and for the beach. Maybe her big sister wouldn't sigh so much if it was a nice day.

Toni and Janie spent the morning at the zoo, but Toni could tell that her sister didn't like it. Janie wanted to get to the beach so that she could get a tan. They hurried past the bears and the tigers and the lions, and then they raced down to the beach.

"Don't bother me!" Janie said when they were settled.

"Don't talk to me. Don't look at me. And whatever you do, don't follow me!"

Janie closed her eyes and let the sun warm her. After a while, Toni went off to look for shells. She walked up and down the beach for a long time. The sun was very hot and she was bored, so she went back to her sister.

"Come in the water with me, Janie," she pleaded. But Janie didn't even open her eyes.

"*Please* Janie," Toni said a few minutes later. "Please come in the water with me."

Janie sighed loudly and stood up. "Look," she said. "I'm going for a walk and I want you to stay right here. Don't go near the water. And whatever you do, *don't* follow me! We'll go in the water when I get back."

She started to walk away, but then she stopped and turned back.

"Wait a minute," Janie said. "I have an idea. Lie down on your back and stay very still."

Toni stretched out in the sand and squinted up at her big sister.

"All right," Janie said. "Now stay exactly like that until I get back. I'm going to put a coin on your forehead. It'd better be right where I put it when I get back."

"Promise you'll go in the water with me if I don't move?" Toni asked.

Janie placed a coin right in the middle of Toni's forehead and smiled. "I promise," she said.

Janie walked down the beach and began to climb. The rocks were high and steep and she climbed for a long time. When she reached the top, she stopped and looked around. She could not see the beach from where she was, so she didn't know if her sister still had the coin on her forehead.

Janie liked it up there. She was all alone, and she liked that. The sun was hot and it was very quiet. She sat on a rock for a long time.

Suddenly a branch snapped.

"Toni?" Janie said.

But no one answered.

Janie stood up and started to climb down the rocks.

Someone was following her. Whenever she stopped, she heard footsteps behind her.

"Toni?" she called again. But still no one answered.

She walked faster, then faster still. The footsteps were closer now. She could hear breathing and panting, and for a moment she wondered if an animal was behind her.

But that was silly. There were no animals around there. Not big ones that breathed loudly and panted.

It was Toni. Her sister was just trying to scare her. "Stop following me, Toni!" Janie shouted. And the footsteps stopped.

Maybe an animal had escaped from the zoo. Maybe a bear or a lion was right behind her.

She hurried, then stopped again. It had to be Toni. It just had to be. "I mean it, Toni!" she shouted, and her words echoed off the rocks.

She took a deep breath and bounded down the rocks. At the bottom, she closed her eyes and sat in the sun. She didn't want her little sister to know that she was scared.

After a while, she strolled down the beach. Toni was lying in the sand with her eyes closed. The coin was still on her forehead.

"Time to go in the water, Toni," Janie said calmly.

They swam for a few minutes, and then they went home. Janie didn't say a word about the footsteps.

But she couldn't stop thinking about them. Who had been following her? Was it Toni?

Janie had her answer at supper that night. She was eating a mouthful of potatoes, when she happened to glance at her sister.

"You're sunburned," Janie said.

"So are you," Toni answered.

Suddenly, Janie's eyes widened, as she noticed something strange on her sister's face.

"You *didn't* follow me," Janie whispered. "The proof is on your forehead."

Toni looked puzzled. "Of course I didn't," she said. "Why? Did someone follow you?".

Janie didn't answer. She was thinking about the footsteps. She was remembering the panting, and the breathing.

How did Janie know that Toni hadn't followed her?
What did she see on her sister's forehead?

20. THE CONTEST

It was the biggest contest the village had ever seen. The Village Toy Shop was giving away a toy. Any toy. And the Village Toy Shop had the best toys in the whole country.

They had kid-sized cars that moved by themselves. They had mountain bikes and racing bikes. They had every kind of game you've ever heard of. And they had robots and pool tables and roller blades.

Everyone in the village wanted to win that contest. The Village Toy Shop announced the contest in the newspaper:

JOIN OUR CONTEST!
WINNER GETS ONE TOY –
CHOOSE THE ONE YOU LIKE!
9 A.M. ON APRIL 16TH.
YOFV YZOOLLM RM HSLK

Steven Browne wanted to win that contest. He had never wanted anything more in all his life. He studied the message in the paper carefully. What did those last four words mean? Maybe they were in code. But what code was it? Or maybe it was a computer error. Steven ripped the message out of the paper. He put it in his jacket pocket and thought about it for a while. Then he forgot all about it.

Every day Steven went down to the Village Toy Shop and looked around.

If he won the contest, he would choose a bike, he thought. But the next day he changed his mind. If he won the contest, he would choose some hockey skates. But the day after that he changed his mind again.

He would choose a chemistry set.

He would choose a ping-pong table.

He would choose a pair of skis.

"How do I win?" he asked the owner, Mrs King.

"Find the balloon," she said. She was busy writing something on a piece of paper.

"What balloon?" Steven asked as he read what she had written.

BLF DRM.

"You'll see," Mrs King said, as she stuffed the paper into a blue balloon. But that is all she would say about the contest.

Steven waited, and while he waited he thought about toys. There were so many wonderful things in that shop.

Which one would he choose?

At 9 a.m. on 16 April , Steven went down to the Village Toy Shop. The street outside was crowded. Everyone in town seemed to be there. They pushed and shoved and waited for Mrs King to come out.

Finally, the door opened and the owner appeared. She went around the corner and came back with five men. The men were holding hundreds of strings that were attached to hundreds of balloons. And on each of the balloons were the words:

The Village Toy Shop
ABC=ZYX

As the crowd cheered, the men let the balloons go. The blue and red and yellow balloons floated away slowly and drifted out of town.

ABC=ZYX, Steven thought. Was it another computer error?

"When you find them, pop them," Mrs King shouted. "And then you'll know."

The crowd raced after the balloons. They ran through the village and they ran out of town.

But it was a fine, windy day, and the balloons were too fast for them. They drifted higher and higher into the sky.

There was nothing to do but wait until the balloons began to lose air. Only then would they come down somewhere.

But Steven didn't run. He stayed right where he was, in front of the Toy Shop, and thought about the letters. As he thought, he glanced through the window of the shop.

Mrs King was holding the string of a blue balloon. She wasn't moving. She was just standing there, waiting for something.

Steven wondered why she didn't come outside and let the balloon go.

Suddenly Steven had an idea. He reached into his jacket pocket and raced into the shop.

So that was it. The key to the code was on the balloons. He unfolded the message and began to write. When he was finished, he popped the blue balloon. There was a small piece of paper inside. Steven read it and smiled. Then he went home to think about what prize to choose.

What did the message in the paper say? What did the paper in the balloon say?

ANSWERS

1. SURPRISE!
When he touched the lamp, he burned his
hand. Someone had just turned the light off.

2. REMOTE CONTROL
Jimmy was ten. His older brother was 12.
Liam pushed the buttons.

3. ONE SMALL DIFFERENCE
Ellen was left-handed.

4. THE GHOST
George brought it in through the flap in the door.

5. THE GOLDFISH
If Diana had put the fish in the glass the
night before, the ice cubes would have melted.

6. THE SNAKE
Jessica had a jacket just like Mary's. Mary took the wrong jacket when the fire bell rang.

7. THE PUDDLE
Jeremy's mother forgot to turn off the bath tap.

8. THE RICH GIRL
Lindy wrote a note. If she had never seen a person, she wouldn't know how.

9. MAKE ME HUMAN, TRUMAN
Janet made Monica's hair green. She was the only one with a blue crayon. When you add blue to yellow, it turns green.

10. THE FLASHING LIGHT
Damon couldn't have known that the torch was red if it was far away. He must have been lying.

11. THE VULTURE
No one can hear anything when the water in the shower is running.

12. THE CASE OF THE JUNK FOOD THIEF
Omar grabbed the open door. There was red paint on his hand, and red paint on the packets of food.

13. THE TRIPLETS

There was freshly-cut hair on Sally's shoulders.

14. THE THING UNDER THE TRAP DOOR

Jake left the room when it got dark. He went down the steps that led to the little open door. Jake was the Thing Under the Trap Door.

15. UP IN SMOKE

The note that was taped to the box wasn't burned. So Jeremy must have put the box in the shop *after* the fire.

16. THE MONSTER IN THE BATHTUB

The water in the bath was very hot at seven. Ellie was in the bathroom just before that.

17. JAMIE'S STORY

Footprints.

18. THE PLANT DID IT!

Pieces of the little king fell onto the newspaper. The date on the newspaper gave Raymond away.

19. FOOTSTEPS

The sun had been shining on Toni while Janie was gone. There was a white circle on Toni's forehead, where the coin had been. So, Toni couldn't have followed her big sister.

20. THE CONTEST

The code was:
ABCDEFGHIJKLMNOPQRSTUVWXYZ=
ZYXWVUTSRQPONMLKJIHGFEDCBA.
So A=Z, B=Y, C=X, and so on.

The message in the paper was:
BLUE BALLOON IN SHOP.

The message in the balloon was:
YOU WIN.